D0416657

Five reasons why you'll LOVE this book:

You'll meet a really
imaginative girl called Polly.

You'll meet her whole family, too.

You'll even meet her friend
(who no one else can see).

The story is full of surprises.

This book is fun to share with
the grown-ups in your life!

For A, J and J.

OXFORD
UNIVERSITY PRESS

Great Clarendon Street, Oxford OX2 6DP

Oxford University Press is a department of the University of Oxford.
It furthers the University's objective of excellence in research, scholarship,
and education by publishing worldwide. Oxford is a registered trade mark of
Oxford University Press in the UK and in certain other countries

Copyright © Rachel Quarry 2019

The moral rights of the author and illustrator have been asserted
Database right Oxford University Press (maker)

First published 2019

All rights reserved. No part of this publication may be reproduced,
stored in a retrieval system, or transmitted, in any form or by any means,
without the prior permission in writing of Oxford University Press,
or as expressly permitted by law, or under terms agreed with the appropriate
reprographics rights organization. Enquiries concerning reproduction
outside the scope of the above should be sent to the Rights Department,
Oxford University Press, at the address above

You must not circulate this book in any other binding or cover
and you must impose this same condition on any acquirer

British Library Cataloguing in Publication Data
Data available

ISBN: 978-0-19-276904-6 (paperback)

1 3 5 7 9 10 8 6 4 2

Printed in China

Paper used in the production of this book is a natural,
recyclable product made from wood grown in sustainable forests.
The manufacturing process conforms to the environmental
regulations of the country of origin.

Polly
and the
New Baby

Rachel Quarry

OXFORD
UNIVERSITY PRESS

Bunny was Polly's friend, but
no one else could see him.

Polly pushed Bunny everywhere
in the pushchair that used to be
hers when she was a tiny baby.

'Why don't you put Bunny in the trolley?'
said Mum at the supermarket.

'He doesn't like sitting with
the shopping,' said Polly.

'Why don't you have a go on your trike?'
said Dad when they were in the park.

'There's no room for Bunny
on my trike,' said Polly.

'Shall we leave the pushchair at home today?' suggested Dad as they were getting ready to go to Gran's house.

'But we need it!' said Polly. 'Bunny loves
to ride around Gran's garden.'

'Do you think Bunny will always need the pushchair?' asked Gran gently.

'Yes,' said Polly.

Mum and Dad were getting worried. They were going to need the pushchair back. Quite soon!

Dad found Bunny a doll's pram at the toy shop.

Too small!

Gran sent Bunny a special carrier.

Too tight!

Mum fixed a trailer to Polly's trike . . .

. . . but the trailer was wobbly.

Bunny's
fallen out!

'It's no good,' whispered Mum.
'Polly just isn't going to give up
the pushchair in time for the new baby.'

When Mum was almost ready to have her baby, Polly and Bunny went to stay at Gran's house.

Polly and Bunny did lots and lots of waiting for the new baby.

Until . . .

'Meet Lily,' said Mum, 'your new sister.'

Polly decided it was time to make
an announcement.

'Bunny can walk!' she said.

'Oh, thank goodness!' said Mum.
'Now baby Lily can have your old pushchair.'

'But what will Bunny's new sister ride in?' said Polly.

'Bunny's new sister?'
said Mum and Dad.

'I know,' said Polly. 'Bunny's new sister
and baby Lily can share the pushchair.'

Bunny and his sister were Polly
and baby Lily's friends . . . but
no one else could see them!